SUSAN MEDDAUGH

sandpiper

HOUGHTON MIFFLIN HARCOURT
BOSTON • NEW YORK

I hope that soup is gone when I come back in there!

For the Finneys

All rights reserved. Published in the United States by Sandpiper,
an imprint of Houghton Mifflin Harcourt Publishing Company,
Boston, Massachusetts. Originally published in hardcover in
the United States by Houghton Mifflin Company, Boston, in 1992.

SANDPIPER and the SANDPIPER logo are trademarks of
the Houghton Mifflin Harcourt Publishing Company.

For information about permission to reproduce selections from
this book, write to Permissions, Houghton Mifflin Company,
215 Park Avenue South, New York, New York 10003.

Library of Congress Cataloging-in-Publication Data

Meddaugh, Susan.
   Martha speaks / Susan Meddaugh.
   p. cm
   Summary: Problems arise when Martha,
   the family dog, learns to speak after eating alphabet soup.
   HC ISBN-13: 978-0-395-63313-7 PA ISBN-13: 978-0-395-72952-6
   [Dogs — Fiction.] I. Title.
   PZ7.M51273Mar1992   91-48455
   {E} —dc20   CIP
                          AC

Manufactured in Singapore
TWP 30 29 28 27 26

The day Helen gave Martha dog her alphabet soup,

something unusual happened.

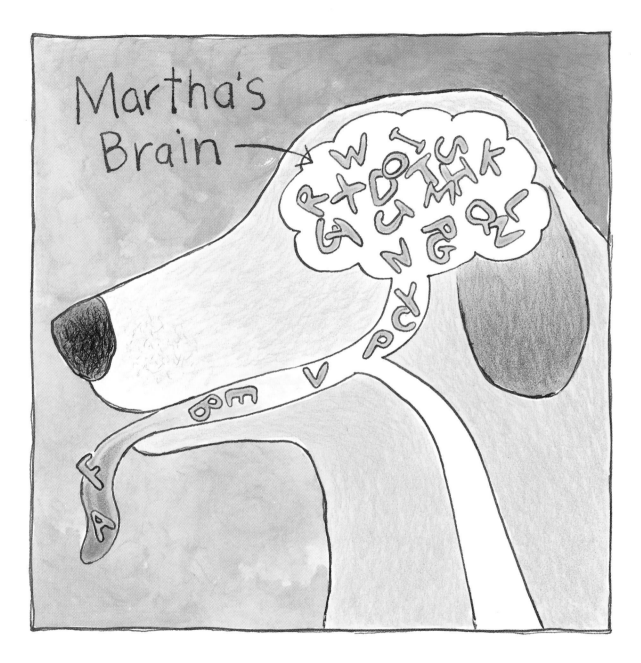

The letters in the soup went up to Martha's brain
instead of down to her stomach.

That evening, Martha spoke.

Martha's family had many questions to ask her.
Of course, she had a lot to tell them!

Alphabet soup became a regular part of Martha's diet,
and the family had a wonderful time surprising people.
Walking the dog was always good for a laugh.

They ordered pizza from a different restaurant every night.

They taught Martha how to use the phone.

But this was a mistake.

Pretty soon, more than pizza was being delivered!

Family and friends were amazed.

Although there were those who doubted,

Martha always had the last word.

But there was a problem:
now that Martha could talk, there was no stopping her.
She said exactly what was on her mind.

She made embarrassing comments.

And, she always told the truth.

Occasionally she wondered why
her family was often mad at her.

But she kept on talking.
She talked through everyone's favorite TV shows,

except her own.

She talked while they were trying to read.

She talked and talked . . .

I was born in a back alley to a poor but loving mother. Although she was a mixed breed, Momma was determined to raise us puppies right, to give us a solid background before we went out into the world at eight weeks. Even before our eyes were open, Momma would say: "You're dogs! Not cats! Don't ever forget that!"

Blah Blah Blah Blah!

Blah Blah Bla

I still remember the rules Momma gave us to live by: ① Beware of Two-year-old humans with clothes-pins. ② Under the table is the very best place to be during a meal. ③ Never mistake your human's leg for a tree.

..Blah..

ah Blah...

Blah Blah...
Blah Blah (that was for my brothers, of course.) And...

Blah Blah Blah ④ if it's black and white and smells funny, it's not a cat. Don't chase it.

Blah Blah Blah
BLah Blah Blah
Blah Blah

And while we're on the subject, I understand Cat, but I can't speak it. Blah

Wait... where was I? Bl

Oh yes.... Blah

Blah Blah Blah B

and talked . . .

until her family could not stand it and said, "Martha, *please!*"

"What's wrong?" asked Martha.
"You talk too much!" yelled Father.
"You never stop!" yelled Mother.
"Sometimes," said Helen,
"I wish you had never learned to talk."

Martha was crushed.

The next day, Martha did not speak. She didn't ask
for her dinner, or to go out. She offered no opinions,
but lay quietly beneath the kitchen table.

At first her family enjoyed the silence, but after
a while they became worried.
"What's the matter, Martha?" asked Helen.
Martha didn't answer.
Helen's father called the vet.
"There's something wrong with my dog!" he said.
"She won't say a word."
"Is this some kind of a joke?" snapped the vet.

Helen offered Martha bowl after bowl of alphabet soup,
but Martha had lost her appetite for letters.

Martha's family wondered if she would ever speak again.

Then one evening when her family was out, Martha heard the sound of glass breaking.

"A burglar!" she gasped. "I better call the police."

She carefully dialed 911.

But when she opened her mouth to speak —

Martha hadn't eaten a bowl of alphabet soup in days!

Martha raced to the kitchen.
She barked. She growled.
She tried to look ferocious.

The burglar wasn't frightened. He picked up a pot from the stove.

"Uh, oh," thought Martha. "It's taps for sure."
But to her surprise, the burglar put the pot down
on the floor in front of her.
"Here, doggy," he said. "Have something nice to eat."

The burglar smiled as he closed Martha into the kitchen
and went back to work.

"Dumb dog," he said.
"Lucky for me you like alphabet soup."

When Martha's family returned, they found the police
removing the burglar from their house.
"How did you know he was robbing our house?" asked Helen.
"We got a call at the station," said the officer.
"Some lady named Martha."

"Good dog, Martha!" exclaimed her happy family.
"You're so right," said Martha.

Now Martha eats a bowl of alphabet soup every day.
She's learning what to say and when to say it, and
sometimes she doesn't say anything at all . . .
at least for a few minutes.